EMERSON SCHOOL

WITHDRAWN

A Spotlight Club Mystery

# Mystery of the Whispering Voice

*Florence Parry Heide*
*and Sylvia Worth Van Clief*

Illustrations by Seymour Fleishman

ALBERT WHITMAN & Company, Chicago

Library of Congress Cataloging in Publication Data

Heide, Florence Parry.
    Mystery of the whispering voice.

    (*Their* A Spotlight Club mystery)   (Pilot books series)
    SUMMARY:  A newcomer to town arouses the suspicion
of the Spotlight Club members with his behavior, his
habit of whispering, and his strange mistakes.
    [1. Mystery and detective stories]   I. Van Clief,
Sylvia Worth, joint author.   II. Fleishman, Seymour,
illus.   III. Title.
PZ7.H36Myn          [Fic]          74–8511
ISBN  0–8075–5389–1

Text © 1974 by Florence Parry Heide
and Sylvia Worth Van Clief
Illustrations © 1974 by Albert Whitman & Company
Published simultaneously in Canada by
George J. McLeod, Limited, Toronto

# Contents

# 1 · The Mysterious Mr. Manchester

IT WAS Jay's first day on his new newspaper route. He had only one more street to go. He turned his bike into Wood Road.

Just then a taxi pulled up beside him. The taxi driver leaned out and said, "Hey, do you know which house is Mr. Chester Manchester's? All this lady knows is that it's on Wood Road. And I see a lot of houses here."

The thin lady in the back seat leaned forward. She clutched a letter in one hand. With the other, she held on to her red hat.

"Road's End," she said, waving the letter at Jay and pointing to the end of the street. "The name of his place is Road's End. So it must be at the end of the road. See, it's a dead-end street. I'm no taxi driver, but even *I* could figure *that* out."

Jay looked at the thin face. Too thin for a smile, he decided. He glanced at his route book. "This is my first day in this neighborhood," he said to the taxi driver. "But I think it *is* that house at the end of this street. The house with the gate across the driveway."

"That's it, that's it," said the lady in the red hat. "Mr. Manchester told me to open the gate and come right in." She pointed to the end of the street. The cab drove off.

Jay had only two customers on Wood Road. He looked at his route book. One was Mrs. G. Mudge. That would be the little white house. Two, that was Mr. Chester Manchester.

The taxi minus the thin lady passed Jay on the way back toward downtown. The driver waved and honked at Jay.

When Jay got to the white house, a round little lady was sitting on the porch swing. She saw Jay and waved. "You're the new newsboy," she said. "Good. I've been waiting for you."

Jay ran up to the porch and handed her the newspaper.

"I'm Mrs. Mudge, rhymes with fudge," said the round lady. "And you can have some fudge every time you come." She pointed to a plate of fudge on a table in front of her.

Jay grinned to himself. Anyone could see that Mrs. Mudge loved fudge.

At that moment Jay heard the driveway gate at the end of the street slam shut. He turned around. The lady in the red hat stood beside the gate. She was carrying a very large handbag. It was almost a suitcase, noted Jay. She looked very angry. Her face was as red as her hat.

The thin lady saw Mrs. Mudge and Jay. Striding over to them she said, "Well, I never!" She shook her head. "Talk about rudeness! And now I'm stuck way out here. A sorry way to treat a lady." Pointing at Mrs. Mudge, she asked, "May I use your telephone? I have to call a taxi." She set her big handbag down.

"Of course," said Mrs. Mudge. "Come right in."

The tall thin lady in the red hat sniffed. She

looked back at the gate. "He hired me to take care of his house. Hired me to be his housekeeper, plain as day."

She reached into her pocket and pulled out the letter she had had in the taxi. She waved it in the air.

"Look! It says right here, *right here*! Plain as day. Four o'clock today, Friday." She turned and glared back at the gate.

Jay glanced at the letter. It was typed, and there was a big scrawled signature at the bottom.

"He just moved in, you know," said Mrs. Mudge. She leaned forward, her eyes wide. "I haven't even seen him yet. Not up close, anyway. What happened?"

"I knocked and I knocked. Then I rang and I rang. Then he came to the door. Acted funny! Said I wasn't to start yet. Wouldn't even let me inside. Wouldn't even let me in to call for a taxi!"

Mrs. Mudge shook her head in sympathy.

"I've a mind not to come back at all," said the thin lady. "But it's a good job. Pays a lot. I already quit my other places." She sniffed and waved the letter again. "He's lucky to get me. He knew it. Said

I was the best housekeeper to answer his ad. I had the best references."

She pointed to her handbag. "I take pride in my work. Even bring my own special polish. My own knee pads. No mops for me. Mops are for slops —sloppy people, I mean. You have to get down on your knees and scrub, with a stiff brush!"

"What happened?" asked Mrs. Mudge again.

The thin lady waved the letter with the large sprawling signature again. "It says here, 'Dear Mrs. Spooner.' It makes everything clear. And now he won't even let me in."

Mrs. Spooner gave a loud sniff and then looked from Jay to her big handbag. "Your boy can carry my bag in," she said. "I don't want anything to happen to it while I'm telephoning."

Mrs. Mudge smiled at Jay. "He's not my boy. He's the newsboy. Not that I couldn't use a boy around here. To cut the grass. Pull the weeds. Run errands. Things like that." She sighed.

"I'll be going," said Jay after he put the bag in the house. "I have to deliver Mr. Manchester's paper."

Mrs. Spooner sniffed. "Mr. Manchester, indeed.

Mr. *Rude*, he is. Not even letting me in to telephone."

She followed Mrs. Mudge into the house.

Jay walked his bike over to Mr. Manchester's gate. There was a big mailbox outside. On it was lettered: Mr. Chester Manchester, Road's End, Wood Road.

Jay propped his bike against the post. He opened the driveway gate and closed it behind him.

The driveway, shaped like a half circle, led up to the front door. The drive was covered with little sharp stones—not too good for bicycle tires.

Jay went up to the door and rang the bell. He wondered if Mr. Manchester would be as rude to him as he had been to Mrs. Spooner. He'd soon find out.

Suddenly there was a commotion at the back of the house. A big shaggy brown dog came loping toward Jay. A little white dog was right behind. They came running up to Jay, tails wagging. Jay leaned down to pet them.

A tall man with a long drooping moustache came running from behind the house. Mr. Manchester, thought Jay.

The man slowed down when he saw Jay with the dogs.

"Glad you stopped them," he said. "I am trying to train those dogs to stay in that pen back there. They're spoiled. They think they can be in the house all the time. I won't have it."

Long, limp hair hung over the man's eyes. He brushed it back and asked, "Who are you?"

"I'm the newsboy, Jay Temple," said Jay. "I just wondered where you'd like me to leave your

newspaper every day. In the mailbox at the gate? Or here at the front door?"

Mr. Manchester tugged at his moustache. "Front door, I suppose," he muttered.

Jay wrote it down. That way any substitute carrier would know where to put it if Jay got sick or was away.

The dogs sat down beside Jay. Mr. Manchester glowered at them. "These dogs are a nuisance, inside and out," he said. "The pen's too small. It needs to be bigger. They bark if I put them in it. What they need is some exercise, somebody to take them out for walks, to tire them out."

Jay wondered why Mr. Manchester had dogs at all if he thought they were a nuisance. He handed Mr. Manchester his route book and a pencil. "I just need your signature. It's the rule when we have a new customer."

Mr. Manchester took the route book. The big brown dog ran off to inspect some bushes.

Jay leaned down to pet the little white dog. "Hey, fella," said Jay, rubbing behind the dog's ears. "You're a nice dog."

"They're just mutts, mongrels, you know. I'm

going to get myself a dog with a pedigree. Expensive, distinguished. A Russian wolfhound, maybe, something like that."

The dogs chased each other around Jay. "What are their names, Mr. Manchester?" asked Jay, petting the little white dog.

The man was signing Jay's route book. "I'm not . . ." he said, then stopped and frowned. He looked at Jay. "I broke the pencil. I have a pen, wait a minute."

He reached into his pocket and pulled out a pen. He signed Jay's route book and handed it back. He pushed the hair out of his eyes. Then he looked around at the big brown dog and shook his head. "Big oaf, that dog," he muttered.

Jay said, "My sister Cindy would be glad to come over every day and take the dogs for a run."

"Good," said Mr. Manchester. "Every morning a long walk, a run in the park. I'll pay her."

"She'd be glad to do it all summer," Jay answered, grinning. Cindy would be glad to have a summer job, he thought. Especially a job that would be so much fun.

"That won't be necessary," said Mr. Manchester. "Just until Wednesday. I'll be gone after that. Have her come tomorrow morning, Saturday. That will be splendid."

He turned and walked toward the back of the house.

Jay frowned. The man had just moved in. Why did he say he'd be gone after Wednesday? And why didn't he like his own dogs?

Jay glanced at his route book before he put it back in his pocket. *Chester Manchester.* Signed in green ink. He stopped and looked at the page again. The writing wasn't at all like the big fancy signature on Mrs. Spooner's letter.

If this was Mr. Manchester's signature, who had signed the letter to Mrs. Spooner?

Jay frowned as he put the route book back in his pocket. If Mr. Manchester had written the letter, why hadn't he remembered that Mrs. Spooner was coming today? Why hadn't he even let her in the house to call a taxi?

And what about the dogs? Why did he have dogs he didn't like?

And what did he mean when he said he'd be gone after Wednesday?

## 2 · Is There Proof in Writing?

JAY CLOSED the gate behind him. He got his bike and walked it over to Mrs. Mudge's house.

Mrs. Spooner was sitting on a straight chair on the front porch. Waiting for the taxi, Jay decided.

"Could I have another look at that letter?" asked Jay. "The one Mr. Manchester wrote to you?"

Mrs. Spooner frowned. Her whole face frowns, thought Jay, not just her forehead. "Why, young man?" she asked sourly, pointing at him. "Don't you believe me?"

"I'm just trying to solve the mystery," said Jay. "The mystery of why Mr. Manchester didn't remember that you were coming today. The mystery of why he wouldn't even let you in to telephone."

Mrs. Spooner said nothing. She pursed her lips. Then she handed Jay the folded letter. Jay opened it and read it quickly. It was typed.

Dear Mrs. Spooner:

I have called your references. I am now well satisfied that you are the housekeeper I want to hire. The terms will be those that were stated in my advertisement in the newspaper.

The job will start on Monday, July 10. However, I will be out of town on that day and will not be able to show you around the house and outline your duties. Will you therefore please come on Friday afternoon at four o'clock? If for any reason you cannot come, please telephone me at this number: 652–1100.

I will look forward to meeting you on Friday, then. Four o'clock sharp, please.

The letter was signed Chester Manchester in the big flourish that Jay remembered. He compared it to the signature signed in green in his route book. The two signatures were entirely different.

Jay looked at the address typed on the corner of the letter.

Road's End, Wood Road
Kenoska, Illinois

He handed the letter to Mrs. Spooner. Mrs. Mudge came back out on the porch.

"Well?" Mrs. Spooner asked, pointing at Jay. "Does that sound like a man who would forget? Does that sound like a man who would turn you away?"

Jay shook his head. "It does seem funny," he said.

"Funny!" snorted Mrs. Spooner. "I don't call rudeness funny. I call it sad! No excuse!" She set her red hat more firmly on her head. "He'll have to mend his ways if he wants *me* to work for him!" she said.

"Are you coming on Monday, then?" asked Jay.

"That's another thing," sniffed Mrs. Spooner. "Now he doesn't want me to start until Wednesday. He says he'll show me around."

Just then a taxi drove up. Mrs. Spooner stood, then she pointed to the taxi. "I hope you're a good driver, young man," she called.

The taxi driver got out of the taxi and saluted. "Good? I'm the best, ma'am," he said.

"Humph," snorted Mrs. Spooner. "I'll decide about that." When she had gone, Mrs. Mudge smiled and started swinging back and forth on the swing. "Talk about rudeness," she said, "Mrs. Spooner didn't even say please or thank you. To either of us."

"I guess she was pretty upset," said Jay. "That Mr. Manchester certainly does seem like a strange man."

Mrs. Mudge nodded. "Yes, he does, doesn't he? And he sounded so nice on the telephone yesterday when I called."

"You called him?" asked Jay.

"Oh, yes. To welcome him to the neighborhood, you know. He said he already loved it. Said it was a wonderful house for him and for his dogs. He said they were his children—the dogs, I mean. That doesn't sound like a rude man."

Jay frowned. "When did he move in, Mrs. Mudge?"

"Oh, the furniture came a week ago. In vans. He'd sent someone ahead to be over there to see that everything was put in the right place. Then Mr. Manchester himself came just day before yesterday. With the dogs."

Mrs. Mudge helped herself to a piece of fudge. "I saw them driving in, that's how I know. Couldn't get a good look at him." She shook her head. "It's hard to believe it's the same man who was so rude to Mrs. Spooner."

Jay was puzzled. Were Mrs. Mudge and Mrs. Spooner both telling the truth? Mr. Manchester did seem to have changed his personality overnight.

Jay rode home. He wanted to think about the last few minutes. He wanted to sort things out in his mind. Most of all he wanted to talk to his sister Cindy and Dexter, his best friend. This looked like another mystery for the Spotlight Club to solve.

When Jay rode into their driveway, Cindy was out on the front porch. She had some pans on the ledge. "I'm drying grapes," she explained. "Making my own raisins. So far they just look like wrinkled grapes."

"Well, let them wrinkle by themselves," said Jay. "Where's Dexter? I want to talk to both of you."

"He just called me from his room," she said, pointing next door. "He's on his way over. He's bringing over the birdseed he planted in the little jars. It's sprouting."

"I've got a mystery," Jay announced.

"Oh, good," said Cindy. "What is it?"

"Hi!" Dexter called, running up the porch steps.

"What is this—a Spotlight meeting?" He looked from Cindy to Jay, who nodded.

Cindy took out her notebook and pencil. "Tell all," she said. Jay quickly told them where he had been.

"One funny thing about it is that Mr. Manchester didn't seem to know Mrs. Spooner was coming today. Even though he had written to her about it. And he wouldn't even let her come in to telephone. Why?"

"Maybe he was afraid she'd see something she wasn't supposed to see," said Dexter, pushing his glasses down on his nose.

"What were you telling us about the way he signed his name?" asked Cindy.

"The letter he wrote to Mrs. Spooner was typed. It was signed *Chester Manchester*. The signature looked kind of like this."

Jay took Cindy's notebook. He flipped to a blank page. He tried to sign the name the way he had seen it on Mrs. Spooner's letter.

"Pretty fancy," said Cindy, looking at it.

"Now look at this," said Jay. He took his route book from his pocket and handed it to Dexter.

Dexter pulled his glasses down on his nose and looked.

"See?" said Jay. "The two signatures don't look anything at all alike."

Cindy studied the green signature in Jay's route book. "What's crossed out here?" she asked.

Jay looked. "He started to sign, then his pencil broke. He took out his pen. I thought he just crossed out the pencil part and then wrote his name in the green ink."

Cindy examined the signature. Then she jumped up and went over to the end of the porch. She held the signature up to the sun. "I can't see what he crossed out," she said. "But look."

She brought the route book back to the steps. "Whatever he started to write, it wasn't Chester Manchester," she said. "You can tell by the letters that poke up and poke down, see?" She pointed. The two boys looked closely.

She took out her notebook. "Look. If you write Chester, and cross it out, it looks like this. What is crossed out has something different at the end. It could be a G. Or a Y."

Jay looked closely. "Lots of things it *could* be, but not Chester."

Dexter nodded. "You're right, Cindy," he said. "He started to write something else."

"I think he started to write another name," said Cindy.

"But why?" asked Jay. "We do have a mystery."

"I've already written a page in my notebook," said Cindy.

"Don't leave anything out," said Dexter. "We don't know what will be important later."

Jay told everything he could remember about Mr. Manchester, about Mrs. Mudge, and about Mrs. Spooner. He told about Mr. Manchester's wanting Cindy to take the dogs for a walk.

"Starting tomorrow," said Jay.

"Oh, good," said Cindy. "A summer job."

"Not exactly," said Jay. "It's just for a few days. Just until Wednesday."

"What happens then?" asked Cindy.

"Well, he said he'd be gone then," said Jay, frowning. "And that's another funny thing."

"Maybe he was crabby today because he was tired or something," said Dexter. "We have to remember Mr. Hooley's rule. We can't just guess from the way things look."

"Well, mystery or no mystery, I want to go over to see the dogs," said Cindy. "What are their names?"

"That's funny," said Jay. "I remember asking him what their names were. And he never told me."

"Let's think up an excuse to go over there— now," said Dexter. "I'd like to look around. Maybe meet Mr. Manchester. And Mrs. Mudge."

"And have some fudge," grinned Jay.

"Remember, it's Friday," said Cindy. "We've all got to help organize that neighborhood picnic the folks have planned for Sunday. We promised."

Jay looked at his watch. "That's right," he said. "I guess we'll have to wait until tomorrow before we go over to Mr. Manchester's."

"I'll copy my notes tonight to make them neater," said Cindy.

"Don't forget any of the clues," warned Jay.

"I hope you remembered to tell us every single thing," answered Cindy. "Sometimes it's the little clues that count."

# 3 · Everybody on the Lookout

THE NEXT MORNING the three Spotlight detectives rode their bikes over to Wood Road.

"I can't wait to meet Mr. Manchester," said Cindy. "And his dogs."

"And Mrs. Mudge," added Dexter.

"Remember," said Jay, "everything we see might be important. Let's keep our eyes and ears open."

"Don't we always?" asked Cindy.

They rode up to Mrs. Mudge's house. She was not on the porch. But her front door was open behind the screen door.

They walked up on the porch and rang the doorbell.

Mrs. Mudge came to the door, drying her hands on a dish towel. "My goodness, it's the paper boy," she said. "And some other children. Are you all going to be delivering the paper?"

"No, Mrs. Mudge," smiled Jay. "This is my sister Cindy Temple, and this is our next door neighbor, Dexter Tate. We have a kind of detective club."

"Well, I have a mystery for you," said Mrs. Mudge. "A mystery about that Mr. Manchester."

She tapped her head. "You know, there is something very, very strange about that man," she said. "His whole personality has changed! It's as if he were someone else entirely."

She looked around at the three detectives. "I'll get us some fudge," she said. "I've just made a fresh batch. You can't solve a mystery on an empty stomach."

She went back into the house. They could hear her humming in the kitchen.

The three detectives sat on the porch. They looked over at the closed gate.

"I've just thought of something," said Cindy, looking at her notes. "Maybe it isn't Mr. Manchester who is the mystery. Maybe it's Mrs. Spooner."

"Mrs. Spooner? Why?" asked Jay.

"Well, she's the one who told you that he had forgotten about her coming. She's the one who told you that he wouldn't let her in to use the telephone. She's the one who showed you the letter with the signature. Maybe she made up the whole thing," said Cindy.

"But why would she do that?" asked Dexter.

"Let me think," said Cindy. She looked at her notebook again. "Maybe Mrs. Spooner just wanted an excuse to get into the house. Maybe she wrote that letter herself. Maybe she signed it herself."

"But why?" asked Jay.

"Let me think," said Cindy. Then she said, "Okay, let's say she *was* hired by Mr. Manchester. And she *was* supposed to start on Monday. But maybe she thought that he was going to be away somewhere on Friday. So maybe she typed the letter to herself, signed his name to it, and took it along with her in case someone caught her."

"Caught her at what?" asked Jay.

"Maybe she planned to sneak in and steal something," said Cindy.

"And take it away in that bag!" said Jay.

Just then Mrs. Mudge came out to the porch. She was carrying a plate of fudge.

"We were just talking about Mrs. Spooner," said Jay. "We're wondering if she could have made it all up. About the letter. Just so she would have an excuse to sneak into the house and take something. If someone came, she could show the letter. Then she found Mr. Manchester was there after all. She had to leave. And she had to make up some story. To explain to us why she was leaving so soon."

Mrs. Mudge stopped swinging and stared at Jay.

"Mrs. Spooner? Now why would she do a thing like that? You might as well suspect me of something!" Her face puckered up. "You don't, do you? Suspect me of anything?"

"Of course not," said Cindy. "We have to try everything, you know. We have to be sure that Mrs. Spooner was telling the truth, that's all."

"She left her bag here," said Mrs. Mudge, looking up at Jay. "That bag is still in my living room."

She shook her head. "Mrs. Spooner. No, I would never suspect her of doing anything bad. But you never know, do you, in mysteries? Sometimes the ones you suspect the least turn out to be crooks." She smiled at them all.

"Good fudge," said Dexter, taking a second piece. "Thanks."

Mrs. Mudge looked serious. "I have to tell you something very strange about Mr. Chester Manchester. His voice was different when I called him this morning. When I called him the other day to welcome him to the neighborhood, he had a deep loud voice. Now he has a *whispering* voice!" She looked at the three detectives in turn.

"Maybe he has a cold," said Dexter, pushing his glasses up on his forehead.

"A cold! A cold doesn't change your whole way of talking! A cold doesn't make you forget everything!" sputtered Mrs. Mudge.

"What did he forget this time?" asked Cindy.

"Just everything!" said Mrs. Mudge. "For instance, when I first called him I told him my name was Mrs. Mudge. And I said, 'You know, it rhymes with fudge.' I say that so it will make it easier for people to remember my name. And he laughed and said, 'Well, Mrs. Mudge, my name is Manchester, rhymes with Chester. Chester Manchester.' "

Jay nodded. "That sounds friendly," he said.

"Yes, so when I called him today and he answered in that whispering voice, I was surprised. I thought maybe I had dialed a wrong number because it didn't sound like him at all. So I said, 'Is this Mr. Chester Manchester?' And he said 'Yes.' And I said that I was the Mrs. Mudge that rhymed with fudge. And he didn't even know what I was talking about! He didn't even talk to me! He said I had a wrong number! And he hung up!"

Her chin quivered. "Rude! And just as I thought I was going to have a nice new friendly neighbor. Someone to pass the time of day with once in a while." She started to swing briskly.

"It does seem strange that he could be so nice one time and so rude another," said Cindy.

"Well, and I'd made him a nice casserole, too," Mrs. Mudge said. "Now I don't know what to do with it." Suddenly she brightened. "Maybe you could all stay for lunch?" she asked, smiling at them. "That way you could keep an eye on things that were happening over there."

"Great!" said Jay.

Cindy jumped up. "I'll go over now to see about taking the dogs for a walk. I want to meet this absentminded Mr. Manchester with the whispering voice."

"Why don't we stay here, Dexter? We could cut Mrs. Mudge's grass for her," suggested Jay.

"Oh, I can't afford to hire anyone. I know the grass needs it," said Mrs. Mudge. "But I only can pay a quarter. Boys won't work for that anymore."

"We will," said Dexter. "We'll do the grass because you're giving us lunch."

"I'll pull the weeds," said Jay.

"Oh, this will be just like a party," said Mrs. Mudge happily. "I'm glad you're going to be having the casserole instead of that absentminded Mr. Manchester."

Cindy started walking over to the gate.

Was Mr. Manchester absentminded? Or was there something else? Why had his personality changed? Why had he forgotten so much?

Cindy opened the gate and walked in. She noted the name and address on the big mailbox: Mr. Chester Manchester, Road's End, Wood Road.

She marked it down in her notebook. She

wanted to be sure to remember every single thing.

A big brown dog came running toward her, tail wagging. He was followed by a little white dog. Cindy stopped to pet them. Then she looked around. Mr. Manchester was not in sight. Suddenly a window slammed shut. Cindy glanced up. No one. She walked up to the front door and rang the bell.

The two dogs stood with her at the door.

In a few minutes the door opened. A tall thin man stood in the doorway. He had a long drooping moustache. He brushed his straight straw-colored hair out of his eyes.

"Are you Mr. Chester Manchester?" asked Cindy.

"Who are you?" he asked. Cindy noticed with surprise that his voice was deep and loud. He didn't whisper at all, the way Mrs. Mudge had said. Maybe this wasn't Mr. Manchester. Maybe Mr. Manchester was somewhere in the house.

"I'm Cindy Temple, and I'm looking for Mr. Manchester," said Cindy.

"Oh, you're the newsboy's sister," the man said. "You were going to take the dogs for a walk this morning." He tugged at his moustache.

"There's nothing much wrong with his memory," Cindy thought quickly to herself.

He looked at the dogs. "I don't want them in the house at night. So I tried putting them in the pen. But they bark. Can't leave them loose in the yard at night—they might dig out, bother the neighbors." He pulled again at his long moustache.

Cindy nodded.

"Go around to the back of the house. Just inside the back door is a little hallway. The leashes are hanging in there."

He turned and started back into the house.

"What about the names?" Cindy asked.

He wheeled and stared at her.

"What do you mean?" he frowned, tugging at his moustache.

"The dogs' names," she said. "What do you call them?"

"Oh," said Mr. Manchester. "Frisco and—Pompom, I think. No, that's not right. Tomtom. Frisco and Tomtom."

Cindy thought to herself, "How strange."

He turned to go back into the house, then stopped as Cindy asked, "But which one's which?"

"The big one is Frisco," said Mr. Manchester. He shut the door.

Cindy turned to the little white dog. "Here, Tomtom," she called. He wagged his tail. But he stayed at the screen door. She said in a louder voice, "Here! Tomtom, come here!"

The big brown dog came running over to her. "That's funny," thought Cindy. "He said the big dog was named Frisco."

She looked at the white dog pawing at the screen door. "Here, Frisco, come here," she called. And the little white dog came running to her.

Cindy tested it out a few more times. Mr. Chester Manchester didn't know which dog was which!

Why didn't he know his own dogs?

Cindy thoughtfully walked to the back of the house. The dogs followed her.

The garage door was open. She looked at the car in the garage. It was a big gray car. It had a Florida license plate, she noticed.

You never knew what was going to be important, thought Cindy.

She walked to the back of the house and

opened the back door. She was in a small hallway with a door that led into the house. It might go right into the kitchen, she thought, or maybe into another hall inside the house.

Cindy wondered if the inside door was kept locked. Probably. The little back hallway was a good place to keep things like leashes for the dogs, boots, an old jacket or two, and a snow shovel in the winter.

As Cindy reached up to take down the two leashes she saw a man's new jacket and a raincoat hanging nearby. A pair of men's boots was on the floor. She took the leashes down from the hooks and started outside.

Then she paused and looked back at the hall. She wanted to be sure to notice any clues. Something that didn't seem at all important now might seem important later. She'd learned that much after helping solve other mysteries.

Something wasn't right. What was it?

She shook her head. Maybe it would come to her later. She opened the door.

Suddenly she knew what had seemed wrong. The jacket and the coat were too small for tall **Mr. Manchester**. So were the boots. Whose were they?

Was there someone else in the house? Someone with a whispering voice?

# 4 · Keeping Track of Clues

JAY AND DEXTER were already working on Mrs. Mudge's grass and weeds when Cindy came through the gate with the dogs.

When they saw her coming, the boys waved and ran over. They patted the dogs.

"We've been waiting to hear what happened," said Dexter, taking his glasses off and wiping them on his shirt.

"First of all," said Cindy, "he doesn't have a whispering voice. Not now, anyway."

"But Mrs. Mudge said that he had this morning, when she called him," said Jay.

"Maybe he was whispering so someone in the house wouldn't hear him," said Cindy. "Anyway,

I've got to tell you the other strange things. He didn't know his own dogs apart. He said the big one was Frisco. And he got the name Tomtom mixed up. He said at first it was Pompom."

"You don't mix up your own dogs' names," said Dexter thoughtfully. "That's for sure."

"Not unless you're terribly absentminded," said Jay. "And he seems to be."

"Well, that's another thing," said Cindy. "He remembered talking to you. He remembered I was coming to take the dogs out. So he's really not that absentminded."

The dogs tugged at the leashes.

"I've got to take them for a walk," she said. "A run. But one other thing. The coats in the back hallway are much too small for him. Someone else must be living there, too."

"Maybe there are *two* men in the house," Dexter guessed. "Mr. Manchester and the man with the whispering voice who answered the phone."

Frisco began to bark and Cindy knew she had to get started. She held back long enough to say, "Someone upstairs slammed a window shut. Keep your eyes open! See you for lunch at noon."

Cindy took the two dogs for a long walk and a run in a nearby park. She looked at her watch. It was almost noon. It was time to take the dogs back to Road's End, back to Mr. Manchester.

Cindy opened Mr. Manchester's gate and walked in. She took off the leashes, and the dogs ran to the front door. They were used to being inside, in the house, she thought. And yet Mr. Manchester said he didn't like them in the house.

Cindy rang the doorbell. Then she knocked. Finally Mr. Manchester came to the door. His hair was in his eyes. He brushed it away.

"I've brought the dogs back," she said.

"Oh, fine," he said. "Here, let me pay you."

"This first time was for nothing," Cindy said.

Mr. Manchester tugged at his moustache.

"Do you need me tomorrow?" asked Cindy. "We're having a neighborhood picnic, but I could come here first."

"No, that's all right," said Mr. Manchester.

"I'll come Monday, then," said Cindy.

Mr. Manchester nodded.

Cindy patted the dogs good-bye. Then she ran over to Mrs. Mudge's. She was starved.

"Lunchtime!" called Jay. "Hurry up so we can talk about the mystery."

Just as they were about to sit down, they heard the sound of a car stopping in front of the house.

"Who can that be?" asked Mrs. Mudge. She walked to the front door and peered out. "It's a taxi!" she called.

The three detectives walked from the kitchen to look.

"It's Mrs. Spooner," said Jay.

"Just the way you described her," whispered Cindy.

The taxi driver had opened the door for Mrs. Spooner. She stepped out of the taxi and then pointed to the driver. "You wait here, young man," she said. "And turn off the meter while I'm here. I won't pay for sitting still."

Then she turned and marched up to the porch. Mrs. Mudge opened the door.

"Good morning, Mrs. Spooner," said Mrs. Mudge. "I expect you've come for your bag."

Mrs. Spooner sniffed. "Not my bag. That stays here until I come back to work for Mr. Manchester. *If* I decide to work for him. No sense in dragging it all the way home and then all the way back again."

Mrs. Mudge hesitated. "Well, did you want to visit, then?" she asked.

"No, I just want to get something out of my bag," Mrs. Spooner said. She peered behind Mrs. Mudge and saw Jay, Cindy, and Dexter.

"You," she said, pointing to Jay. "Lift my bag out here."

Mrs. Spooner turned her back to Mrs. Mudge and the detectives. She unzipped the bag, rummaged around in it, and then zipped it shut again. She reached into her pocket and took out a key and a small padlock. She locked the bag shut. Then she sniffed again and put the key back in her pocket.

She turned around and pointed to Jay. "Put the bag inside until I'm ready for it again," she said. After that she turned and walked back to the taxi.

Dexter whistled. "She'll never win any gold stars for politeness," he said.

"What was that all about?" asked Cindy. "She didn't take anything out of the bag at all. She just wanted to lock it up."

Mrs. Mudge sighed. "So I wouldn't peek in it, I suppose," she said.

Jay frowned. "There must be something in there she didn't want us to see," he said. "Can it be something to do with Mr. Manchester? Did he give her something? Or did she take something?"

Mrs. Mudge shook her head. "She didn't steal anything. I know, because I did peek in. I shouldn't have, but I did. I had to be sure. There are only cleaning supplies, just the way she said."

She looked at the three detectives. "You're thinking that was snoopy of me," she said.

Cindy smiled. "No, we're thinking it was lucky for us that you did peek in. That's one less mystery we have to worry about. Unless maybe Mrs. Spooner is very clever and really hid something."

Jay looked at the padlock. "We won't know now. Isn't it time to eat?"

The four of them had lunch. "That was wonderful," said Jay.

"Perfect," added Dexter.

"Delicious," sighed Cindy.

"I'm glad you liked it," said Mrs. Mudge. "Now let's talk about Mr. Manchester."

They sat around the kitchen table.

"I've copied everything over," said Cindy, taking out her notebook. "Listen to this." She read out loud:

*Mystery of Chester Manchester*
*Clues and Questions*

*Mrs. Spooner: Why did Mr. M. forget*
*about their appointment? Why*
*wouldn't he let Mrs. S. in the*
*house to telephone?*
*Query: Was she telling the truth?*
*Or was she making it up?*
*Query: Could Mrs. S. have written*
*and signed the letter*
*herself? So she would have*
*an excuse to get in and*
*maybe steal something*
*when Mr. M. wasn't there.*

"Oh, dear," said Mrs. Mudge. "We shouldn't even think thoughts like that."

Dexter said, "We have to think about anything that might happen. Mrs. Spooner might want to take something. We don't know."

"What's this 'query' bit?" Jay asked Cindy.

"It's my new system. We don't want to miss anything."

"A very good system," said Mrs. Mudge. "A query is a question."

Cindy continued reading.

His voice: Why was he whispering on the telephone when Mrs. Mudge called?

Query: Why had he forgotten about the casserole?

Mrs. Mudge leaned forward. Her blue eyes were round and wide. "Query," she said. "Was Mrs. Mudge telling the truth?" She looked around anxiously. "You have to do that, you know. You have to suspect everybody. Even me. I read lots of mysteries. And almost every time they make someone who is innocent seem suspicious."

"But we don't suspect you of anything, Mrs. Mudge," objected Cindy.

"You should," said Mrs. Mudge. "I could have lied about his whispering voice. And about his forgetting the casserole. You have only my word."

"But we believe you," said Cindy.

"Besides," said Jay, "you wouldn't have any reason to make up something like that."

"Of course not," nodded Mrs. Mudge. "But I'll feel better when someone besides me tells you about his whispering. Then it will be a real clue."

Cindy smiled at Mrs. Mudge. Then she started reading again.

*Query: Was he whispering because he didn't want someone who was in the house to hear him?*

"Who could the someone be?" said Mrs. Mudge. Cindy turned a page in her notebook.

*Dogs: If Mr. M. doesn't like dogs, why does he have them?*
*Query: Why did he tell Mrs. Mudge he felt the dogs were his children?*

— "Oh, dear," said Mrs. Mudge. "How do you know that I didn't make that up?" She glanced around the table.

"Keep reading, Cindy," said Jay. He looked over at Mrs. Mudge. Cindy read from her notes.

*Query: Why doesn't he know his own dogs' names? Why doesn't he know which is which?*

*Query: Does he have them for watchdogs?*

Jay shook his head. "If you have dogs for watchdogs, you have dogs that bark. Or growl. Or something."

"That's right," nodded Dexter. "At least they should look fierce."

"What else?" asked Jay.

"One more thing," said Cindy, reading.

*Clothes: Why are the clothes hanging in the back hallway much too small for Mr. M.? Whose are they?*

"Maybe he's still growing," grinned Dexter. "Maybe those were his last year's clothes."

Jay picked up Cindy's notebook and studied it. "Funny," he said after a moment. "It almost seems as if there are *two* Mr. Manchesters. Maybe someone else is over there."

"Right," agreed Dexter. "Maybe Mrs. Mudge's Mr. Manchester is over there. The Mr. Manchester who can wear the small coat and boots. The Mr. Manchester who is friendly and polite."

Jay said, "But what about our Mr. Manchester —the man we've met? He isn't any of those things. Who is he? A real Mr. Manchester, too?"

"Or is he just pretending to be a Mr. Manchester?" asked Cindy, frowning as she spoke.

"Why would anyone do a thing like that?" asked Mrs. Mudge.

"We don't know yet," said Jay. "But there is something fishy about this Mr. Manchester."

"Don't forget Mr. Hooley's rule," said Cindy.

"Who's Mr. Hooley?" asked Mrs. Mudge.

"There isn't such a person, really," said Dexter. "We made him up."

Mrs. Mudge nodded.

"A made-up name for a made-up person," she said.

"We pretended a million dollars was stolen," said Jay. "And it was found in Mr. Hooley's basement. But that doesn't prove he stole it."

"A million dollars?" said Mrs. Mudge. "Who did steal it? And how did they go about it?"

"Nobody really stole it," said Dexter.

"Then how did it get there?" asked Mrs. Mudge.

"We made up the whole thing," said Dexter, pulling at his glasses.

"Made it up?" said Mrs. Mudge. "Think of

that. But wouldn't that get your Mr. Hooley in trouble?"

Cindy smiled. "We made up everything," said Cindy. "There isn't a Mr. Hooley and there never was. And there was never a million dollars in his basement."

Mrs. Mudge nodded. "I see it now," she said. "There isn't a Mr. Hooley, but there is a Mr. Hooley's rule."

"I write everything down in here," said Cindy, holding up her notebook. "But we have to prove everything we suspect."

Mrs. Mudge nodded. "Very sensible," she said. "I can help, too. I see almost everything that happens in this street. Sometimes something happens that doesn't seem a bit important. Then later it does." She looked up at Cindy. "For instance, he drives a red sports car. Drove it the day he moved in. Now maybe that doesn't seem important now. Later maybe it will be a clue."

Cindy stared at Mrs. Mudge. "A red sports car?" she asked. "Are you sure?"

"Of course. He had the dogs in the back seat. I didn't get a good look at him because the big dog was hanging over him, kind of looking out, the way dogs do. Anyway, that's what he came in. A red sports car."

"Well, it isn't there now," said Cindy. "The only car there is a big gray car. With a Florida license."

The three detectives looked at each other. Then they looked at Mrs. Mudge. She looked at her hands. "The red one had a California license," she said. "I always notice things like that."

Where was the red sports car?

"He couldn't drive two cars at the same time," said Cindy.

"Someone must have driven away in the red car!" said Jay. "The important thing is for us to pretend we don't notice anything. If he thinks we suspect him, it will be hard to find out anything."

"You're right," nodded Mrs. Mudge. "Make people think that you believe they're innocent. That way you can find out things."

"Well, we have a good way of keeping an eye on him," said Cindy. "I'll be taking the dogs out—at least until Wednesday."

"And I'll be delivering papers," said Jay.

"And I'll be pulling Mrs. Mudge's weeds and eating her fudge," laughed Dexter.

"There's a good supply of both," smiled Mrs. Mudge. She started swinging again. "I'll be sitting and swinging on my porch. And spying. I hope we don't solve the mystery too soon. It's fun to have young people around again. Are you coming back tomorrow?"

"Well, tomorrow's Sunday," said Cindy. "And our parents have all been planning a big neighborhood picnic. We've been helping with it. And we promised we'd help all day tomorrow. But we'll be back on Monday."

"Your picnic sounds lovely," said Mrs. Mudge. "Maybe after we solve this mystery, we could have a big neighborhood picnic here. But we won't invite the rude Mr. Manchester! Just the nice one." She added, "That will show him!"

It did seem that there might be two Mr. Manchesters, thought the detectives.

One the real one. One a fake?

How could they find out?

# 5 · That Whispering Voice

THE SUNDAY neighborhood picnic was a great success. Neighbors as well as friends from other parts of town were there. The street was blocked off. Children, parents, grandparents were all eating and laughing and having a happy time.

After the party, Dexter's sister Anne helped the three detectives with the dishes. "I'll drive around if you run in with the pie tins and salad bowls and everything," said Anne. "People have put their names and addresses on their dishes with adhesive tape."

The four of them all piled in the car with the remaining platters and bowls. By the time they had delivered the last one, it was dark.

"It looks like a storm coming up," said Anne.

The car was just turning a corner near a small park when Jay said, "Hey! Isn't that Mr. Chester Manchester?"

Dexter and Cindy turned to look.

"Let us out," said Dexter hurriedly. "Don't let him see us."

Anne finished turning the corner and stopped the car. The three Spotlighters jumped out. "Tell everyone we'll be home soon," said Dexter. "We just have to see where he's going."

"You're the friendly neighborhood spies," laughed Anne. "Well, don't ask me to come and pick you up later. I'll be washing my hair. Even if there's a telephone booth over there, don't call me to come to get you. And don't get caught in the rain."

Anne waved and drove off.

By now Mr. Manchester was walking swiftly toward the three detectives.

"Don't let him see us," hissed Jay. Cindy ducked behind a tree, and Jay and Dexter crouched behind nearby bushes. No one else was in the little park.

They watched as Mr. Manchester walked to the

telephone booth. He opened its hinged door.

Jay whispered to Dexter, "His phone must be out of order."

"Maybe," whispered Dexter.

Mr. Manchester closed the door of the booth behind him.

The three dectectives watched. They could see him clearly in the telephone booth. The street light gave his face a strange greenish color. Shadows played across his face. His long drooping moustache looked sinister in the night.

He put one coin in the slot, then another and another. Cindy watched closely. "He's calling long distance," she decided.

He put the receiver between his shoulder and his ear and took out a folded newspaper. Then he took a pen from his pocket and wrote something. Cindy stretched her neck to see. He was writing on the back of the telephone book.

Then as they watched, he pulled a handkerchief from his pocket. They stared as he put it over the mouthpiece.

They stayed, frozen to the spot, as he talked into the telephone. Through the handkerchief.

Cindy felt her heart pounding. Why would he talk through a handkerchief? Why, unless he was trying to disguise his voice?

In a few minutes Mr. Manchester hung up. He folded his handkerchief and put it back into his pocket. Then he tore a piece from the newspaper and put the piece of paper in his pocket. He pushed his long hair out of his eyes. Then he opened the door and started to walk away, pulling at his moustache.

The three detectives waited. When they thought it was safe, they followed him, silently. The wind was just starting to blow.

He walked home. Back to Wood Road. Back to Road's End. And he shut the gate.

Jay, Dexter, and Cindy stood there in the dark.

"Why did he disguise his voice?" whispered Cindy.

"And who was he calling?" frowned Dexter.

"And why did he use a telephone booth?" asked Jay.

They looked toward Mr. Manchester's house, but they could see nothing. They heard a shutter banging. Cindy shivered.

Jay suddenly turned. "He tore something out of that newspaper," he whispered. "But I didn't see him leave with the rest of the paper. Remember, he had it tucked under his arm when he went into the phone booth? He must have left it there."

"But he tore out the important part," objected Dexter, pushing his glasses up. "What good would it do to find the rest? The real clue is in his pocket."

"Let's go back and look for it," urged Cindy. "Maybe we can tell what he did tear out. We'll see what section of the paper it was, anyway."

The three looked through the dark night at Mr. Manchester's house once again. A flickering light moved from window to window.

"Funny, the dogs aren't barking or anything," said Cindy.

"Let's go," said Jay.

The detectives ran through the night, back to the telephone booth where they had seen Mr. Manchester. On the floor of the booth was a folded newspaper. Dexter picked it up and pulled his glasses down on his nose.

"It's one of today's Chicago papers," he said. He turned it over. "Something's been torn out right

here, see? Something from the want ads."

Cindy and Jay looked over his shoulder.

"We get that Sunday paper at home," said Jay. "Let's go home and take a look at it. We can figure out what it was he tore out."

"And maybe find out who he was calling," said Dexter.

The rain started. They turned and ran.

"Who he was calling—and why," panted Cindy.

"And why he tried to disguise his voice," added Dexter.

"Remember Mr. Hooley's rule," said Jay when they stopped running. "We don't know he was trying to disguise his voice with that handkerchief. Maybe he just didn't want to get any germs."

In a few minutes the three detectives were running up the steps of the Temple house.

Mrs. Temple came in from the kitchen.

"Mom, where is today's Chicago paper?" asked Cindy.

"Curled up on the couch," said Mrs. Temple.

Jay picked it up. He and Cindy and Dexter quickly leafed through the newspaper until they came to the want ad section. They spread it out on the floor. They turned the pages carefully.

"Try page four," said Cindy, glancing at the newspaper they had found in the phone booth.

"Here it is," said Jay. They put the page that had been torn on top of the one that was just like it. Cindy took out her pencil. She outlined the hole on the newspaper to show what had been torn out.

"Now," she said, "in this outline is just what Mr. Manchester tore out of the paper tonight."

She looked closely and groaned. "So many numbers! So many ads! How can we ever find out which number he called? It's just like looking for a needle in a haystack."

"Let me see," said Jay. He knelt over the paper.

"Me, too," added Dexter, pushing his glasses down on his nose. He looked at it and whistled. "We'll never be able to find out who he called. Not in a million years!"

Suddenly Cindy brightened. "I remember something," she said. "I remember that he wrote a number on the cover of the phone book or something."

The boys looked at Cindy. "Let's go back," said Jay. "If we find the number that he wrote down, we can find the ad that goes with it. Then we'll know who it was he called."

"That long walk—again?" groaned Dexter. "In the rain?"

"Think we can talk Mom into letting us go out?" asked Jay. "It's late."

"It will be a lot easier to talk Mom into letting us walk than it will be to talk Anne into driving us over," sighed Jay. "You go ask her, Cindy. You're better at things like that."

"It's because I understand women better than you two do," laughed Cindy.

In a few minutes Cindy ran downstairs again. "I love our mother," she said. "She's going to drive us over. She said she'd rather drive than worry."

Mrs. Temple came downstairs in a moment. "You promised this would be a short errand, remember," she said. "I just washed my hair and it's still wet. Besides, it's raining. A storm's in the air."

"This must be hair-washing night," grinned Jay.

They all piled into the car. In a few minutes they were at the telephone booth.

Cindy, Jay, and Dexter scrambled out and ran in the rain over to the booth.

Jay picked up the telephone book and peered at it. Then he groaned. "Maybe the number is here," he announced, "but so are about fifty other numbers. How will we ever know which one it is?"

Cindy frowned at the numbers. "Wait a minute," she said. "Didn't he sign your route book with green ink?"

Jay nodded.

"Well, here's a number in green ink," said Cindy, pointing to the telephone book cover. She took the newspaper page from her pocket. "Wait a minute," she said. "If I can find the same number that is written in green ink here in the newspaper— then that's it!"

Mrs. Temple honked. "This is the operator, your three minutes are up," she announced.

Jay ran over to the car. "Just one second, Mom," he said. "We've almost got it."

In a few minutes Cindy shouted, "Here it is!"

Sure enough. The telephone numbers matched.

"What was that about a needle in a haystack?" grinned Dexter, pushing his glasses up on his head.

Cindy drew a circle around the number in the newspaper.

"What is the ad?" asked Dexter, pulling his glasses down.

"Let's look," said Jay.

"Come on, kids," urged Mrs. Temple. "It's raining. There's going to be a storm. And my hair is catching cold."

"We can look when we get home," said Dexter. They ran over to the car.

"It's something about stamps," said Cindy.

"Stamps?" echoed Jay. "What does he want with stamps?"

"Maybe he wants to write a lot of letters," laughed Cindy.

As soon as the detectives were home again, they studied the ad.

RARE STAMPS WANTED! PRIVATE COLLECTOR searching for following stamps, must be perfect condition, full original gum. Premium prices. Columbus issue . . .

There was a long list of stamps wanted. And at the end, "Call 888-9090, New York City, between 6 and 8 pm, Sunday only."

"Rare stamps," said Jay thoughtfully. "Dexter, you're the stamp collector. What's it all about?"

Dexter shook his head. "I only have a beginning collection," he said. "But full original gum means that nobody's licked it or used a stamp hinge to mount the stamp in an album."

Cindy opened her notebook. "Mr. Manchester just wants to sell some rare stamps," she said. "There's nothing wrong with that."

Dexter spoke up. "There's nothing wrong with it—*if* he owns the rare stamps in the first place."

Cindy glanced up. "You mean he could be trying to sell something that doesn't belong to him?"

"Well," Dexter said, setting his jaw stubbornly, "there are so many things we don't understand about about Mr. Manchester. Is he really Mr. Manchester? It doesn't seem as if the dogs are his. Maybe the stamps aren't either."

"But how can we find out?" asked Cindy. "Remember Mr. Hooley's rule. We don't know for sure that this isn't Mr. Manchester. We're just guessing."

"Maybe we should call this stamp collector in New York," suggested Cindy. "We could warn him that something is wrong."

"We can't. Not until we're sure that something is wrong," argued Jay. "Besides, we can't reach him until next Sunday. The ad says between 6 and 8 pm, Sunday only."

"If this is not the real Mr. Chester Manchester," said Dexter, "where is the real one? In the house? Gone away in the red car Mrs. Mudge saw? Where *is* the real one? And who is this we've been watching?"

"It's funny," said Cindy. "Usually when we try to solve mysteries we know what's been done that's wrong, but we don't know who did it. This time we know who did it, or we think we do, but we don't know what he's done."

"Yet," said Jay.

The three detectives looked at each other.

Then suddenly there was a loud clap of thunder. The lights flickered. Cindy shivered. "I'm scared," she admitted. "Not of the storm, I love them. But I'm scared about the mysterious Mr. Manchester."

# 6 · *On Frisco's Trail*

It RAINED all night. The wind moaned through the trees. Cindy sat up in bed. She thought about Frisco and Tomtom.

"If he's left them out in that pen," Cindy worried to herself. She tossed and turned, thinking about the dogs and about Mr. Manchester.

The next morning she jumped out of bed. The storm was over. She had to get over to see the dogs. She looked out the window. Broken branches from the trees were on the grass. It must have been quite a storm.

Jay and Dexter had to pick up the branches before they could go over to Road's End. Cindy promised to meet them at Mrs. Mudge's as soon as they were finished.

She rode her bike over to Wood Road. She stopped first to say hello to Mrs. Mudge. She knocked on the door, but there was no answer. She must have gone shopping, Cindy decided. She ran over to the gate to Mr. Manchester's house. She opened the gate. The dogs were nowhere in sight.

She ran up the steps of the house and rang the front doorbell. Mr. Manchester came to the door, his hair in his eyes.

"Oh, it's you!" he said, pushing his hair back.

"Are the dogs all right?" asked Cindy. "It was such a storm. I worried about them."

"They're all right," said Mr. Manchester. "They got sick on Saturday. I took them over to the vet's. Maybe they ate something that didn't agree with them, something like that."

"Sick?" asked Cindy. "Oh, dear. But I'm glad they weren't out in that storm."

"You know how dogs are. Always ailing," said Mr. Manchester. "But here, let me pay you for taking them out on Saturday."

"Oh, no, Mr. Manchester," said Cindy. "I did it because I like dogs."

"Well, thank you then," said Mr. Manchester.

"As soon as they're better I can take them out again," Cindy said.

Mr. Manchester pulled on his moustache. "Could your brother come over and help pick up branches this morning?" he asked. "They're all over the place. Blocking my car, too."

"I'm sure he'd be glad to. His friend Dexter could help," said Cindy.

Mr. Manchester nodded and turned to go back into the house.

"Oh, Mr. Manchester, which vet did you take the dogs to?" asked Cindy. "I could go to see them."

Mr. Manchester frowned. "That won't be necessary," he said. He shut the door.

Cindy turned to go. It was too bad the dogs were sick. And it was funny that Mr. Manchester didn't want her to go to see them, or even want her to know where they were. Had he really taken them to the vet's?

She shut the gate hard and started to walk over to Mrs. Mudge's house.

Mrs. Mudge was coming down the street, carrying a grocery bag. Cindy ran to help her.

"Fixings for lunch, in case you can all stay,"

smiled Mrs. Mudge. "Wasn't that a storm?"

"Terrible," agreed Cindy. "I worried about those dogs. But they weren't outside after all. Mr. Manchester took them to the vet's. They were sick."

"Sick!" scoffed Mrs. Mudge as they carried the groceries into the kitchen. "Those dogs weren't any sicker than I am now! I saw him leave with them late Saturday afternoon. In that gray car. The dogs were frisky as anything."

Cindy put the groceries down on the kitchen table. What Mrs. Mudge reported did not agree at all with what Mr. Manchester had said. If the dogs were not sick, then why had he taken them to the vet's? Suddenly a new idea popped into Cindy's head. Had he taken them to the vet's at all? She didn't dare ask Mr. Manchester any more questions. She'd have to find out for herself.

Cindy decided what to do. Suppose he had taken the dogs to the vet's. She could follow up that idea first. "Mrs. Mudge," she said, "May I use your phone book? There must be a list of vets in it."

"Help yourself," Mrs. Mudge answered. "I'll fix a little snack. When are the boys coming?"

"They're picking up branches at home," said

Cindy. "They can pick up your branches, too. And Mr. Manchester wants them to pick up his."

"Good," nodded Mrs. Mudge. "That way they can spy."

Cindy smiled. "You'd make a good detective." She opened the telephone book to the yellow pages. "Veterinarians," she said. "There are five."

"Call them and see if one of them has the dogs," Mrs. Mudge said.

A few minutes later Cindy put the phone down. "Not one vet has any dogs belonging to Mr. Manchester. What can he have done with Frisco and Tomtom?"

"Maybe he got rid of them," said Mrs. Mudge. "Left them on a country road."

"He couldn't do that!" objected Cindy. "He didn't like them, but he did take good care of them."

Why had that man lied about taking the dogs to the vet's? What had he done with them? Slowly Cindy took out her notebook.

"I've thought of something!" she said. "I did call all the vets. And they said no Mr. Chester Manchester had left any dogs. But I didn't ask if anyone had brought in a brown dog and a little white one Saturday. What if he used a phony name?"

Mrs. Mudge raised her eyebrows. "Try that," she said. "It would be just like that Mr. Manchester not to give his name."

Cindy ran into the kitchen. She made three calls. No one had dogs like Frisco and Tomtom. Her heart sank. But she wasn't ready to give up.

She dialed a fourth time. "Is this Dr. Merrick's office?" she asked. "I called a few minutes ago about Mr. Manchester's dogs."

"Oh, yes," said the woman. "They're not here."

"But did anyone bring in a big brown dog and a little white one on Saturday afternoon?"

"Oh, yes. Those dogs are here. They're nice dogs."

"How are they?" asked Cindy.

"In the best of health. Mr. Flamm said he wanted to board them for a few days. He'll get them on Wednesday morning."

Cindy swallowed. "Mr. Flamm?" she asked.

"Yes, Mr. Harry Flamm. He brought them Saturday."

Cindy looked at the telephone. Then she asked, "Is Mr. Flamm a tall man with a moustache?"

"And long hair," said the woman. "Like a sheep dog."

"Thank you," said Cindy and hung up. She ran back to the porch. "I found the dogs! Mr. Manchester used a different name—he told the vet he was Mr. Harry Flamm."

"But who is Harry Flamm?" asked Mrs. Mudge, looking over at the gate. "And why is he pretending to be Mr. Manchester?"

"I don't know yet," admitted Cindy. "But we'll know by tonight. For sure!"

She looked around. "I wish the boys were here," she said.

"Your wish came true," laughed Mrs. Mudge. "Here they come." Sure enough, Dexter and Jay were just turning the corner.

Cindy jumped up. "He's not Mr. Chester Manchester!" she said, as soon as they were close enough to hear. "He's Harry Flamm!"

The boys put their brakes on and skidded to a stop. Then they jumped off their bikes and hurried toward Cindy.

"What? How do you know? What happened?" asked Dexter, pushing his glasses up.

Cindy quickly explained her telephone call to the veterinarian.

"But who is Harry Flamm?" asked Jay. "Why does he say he's Mr. Manchester?" He paused for a moment. Then he reached into his pocket and took out his newspaper route book. "Look. He signed here, remember? He signed something first, and then he crossed it out."

They all looked at Jay's route book. They looked at the signature of Mr. Chester Manchester.

Jay pointed to what had been crossed out. "See? He had started to sign *Harry Flamm*," said Jay excitedly. "Then he crossed it out. And signed *Chester Manchester!*"

They studied the signature.

"You're right, Jay," said Dexter. "That man isn't Mr. Manchester at all! He's Harry Flamm!"

"But who is Harry Flamm?" asked Cindy. "And why is he pretending to be Mr. Manchester?"

"And where is Chester Manchester right now?" asked Jay. "What has Harry Flamm done with him?"

Dexter said, "I think the real Mr. Manchester must be in the house. That's why Mr. Flamm used the phone booth in the park. He didn't want to be overheard."

The three detectives looked over at the house. "But if Mr. Manchester—the real one—is there, he must know that Mr. Flamm took the dogs away someplace. I don't understand at all," Jay said.

Then Cindy remembered. "Whoever that man over there is, he wants you to pick up his branches."

"We've got to find out what's going on—right away," said Dexter. "Let's go. If the real Chester Manchester is over there, we'll find him."

# 7 · *Clue at Crisp's Corner*

THE BOYS started to run toward the gate. Cindy frowned and shook her head. She was worried. What if they got into trouble with Harry Flamm?

She took the folded piece of newspaper from her notebook and spread it out on her lap. "There must be another clue here somewhere," she said, half to herself, half to Mrs. Mudge.

"Yes, but clues are hard to find," said Mrs. Mudge. "Sometimes a clue doesn't look like a clue until it's too late. You can be looking right at one and not know it."

"I know," said Cindy. She studied the piece of paper. "Look," she said. "Here's another ad about rare stamps. And it's right here in Kenoska, too."

Mrs. Mudge looked over Cindy's shoulder. "Hmmm," she said. "He might have tried that one, too. Especially since it's handy. He might have tried several places. Shop around, that's what I always say."

Cindy read the ad out loud.

**CRISP'S CORNER**
For Rare Stamps
We buy and sell
Our Motto:
We buy the best
We sell the best
Let the rest
have second best!
111 Bodd Way,
Kenoska, Illinois
Homer Crisp, Prop.

"Crisp, Crisp, Crisp," muttered Cindy. "That's where Dexter bought his stamps last summer." She put the ad in her pocket. "I'm going there to see what I can find out," she announced.

"That's a good idea," nodded Mrs. Mudge. "But there's probably just one chance in a million that you'll find a real clue."

"I know," agreed Cindy. "But that's what detective work is all about. That one chance."

Cindy ran to her bike.

"I'll have lunch ready for you all at noon," called Mrs. Mudge.

"Wonderful!" said Cindy. "You're spoiling us!"

She had no trouble finding Crisp's Corner. The shop was in a little out-of-the-way street. She parked her bike outside and went in.

The shop was pleasantly musty, like an old bookstore. As she opened the door, a bell tinkled. A tiny old man came from the back of the shop. He was very stooped and walked with a cane.

Cindy wondered where to begin. She thought for a moment, and then she said, "Mr. Crisp, do you have a customer named Chester Manchester? Or one named Harry Flamm?"

Mr. Crisp frowned and shook his head. "No," he said. "I'd know if they were my customers. I don't have very many customers, you see. Just a very few. Not many people want to buy stamps as expensive as mine.

Cindy looked around the shop.

"Of course I do have a few inexpensive stamps for beginning collectors. I'd be happy to show you some of those."

Cindy shook her head, and Mr. Crisp went on,

"Most of my stamps are very expensive indeed. They're worth it. But not many people have that much money to spend on rare stamps. Most people just buy regular stamps, you know." He sighed and rubbed his chin.

"I'm sorry you don't have many customers," said Cindy. "And I'm sorry that I'm not even a customer. I don't want to buy any stamps. I just want to ask you some questions."

"I'll be happy to help you if I can," nodded the old man. "I love to talk about stamps."

Cindy took the newspaper clipping from her pocket.

"There was an ad in yesterday's Chicago

paper," she said. "Sunday's want ad section. It was a private collector. He was looking for some special stamps. Did you see his ad?" Cindy showed the clipping to Mr. Crisp. He studied it.

"Oh, yes, I saw it. In fact, I called him up last night."

"You did?" asked Cindy.

"Yes, indeed. I watch for things like this. That's part of my business. If anyone wants to buy valuable stamps from me, I am here to sell the stamps. If someone wants to sell me some stamps, I am here to buy them." He sighed.

"Tell me about your telephone call, please," said Cindy. "It's very important. You see it's a mystery we're trying to solve."

"Well, as I say, I'm happy to talk about stamps. The man's name is Mr. Higginsby. I have heard his name before. He is a wealthy man and a fussy man. He collects only certain things. But when he wants some special stamps, he is willing to pay a great deal of money."

"I see," nodded Cindy.

"So, I have some of the things he wanted. And I told him about some other very fine stamps I have.

He was interested. I will arrange for him to see my stamps. If he likes them, he will buy them. As I say, he is a rich man. I will be happy to have Mr. Higginsby as a customer. He travels a great deal—in fact he is leaving this morning for a long trip."

"Is there anything else you can tell me?" asked Cindy.

"I wish I could help you," said Mr. Crisp kindly. "As far as stamps go, I could talk all day. But as to your friends Mr. Flamm and Mr. Manchester, I can't say a word because I never even heard of them."

Cindy looked so disappointed that Mr. Crisp though a moment and then exclaimed, "Wait! It's a small world! When I called Mr. Higginsby last night he was surprised to find there were two people in one little town in Illinois interested in rare stamps."

Cindy's heart pounded. "Two people?" she repeated. "You and who else? Who is the other one?"

"I didn't ask, and of course he didn't say," answered little Mr. Crisp. "Sometimes people don't like to have their names given out. They don't want it known that they have a valuable stamp collection.

Or they don't want it known that they are selling some of it."

"Did he say anything else about the other person? The other person from Kenoska?"

Mr. Crisp puzzled a moment. "He said that someone had just called him. He said he had dealt with him before. Sometimes Mr. Higginsby sells stamps to this man. But Mr. Higginsby never bought anything from him before. And that's because this Kenoska man has never wanted to sell his stamps before."

Cindy swallowed. "But he wants to sell them now?" she asked.

Mr. Crisp nodded. "He is very anxious to sell a great many stamps," said Mr. Crisp.

Cindy frowned. "Do you remember anything else?" she asked.

Mr. Crisp paused. "No, nothing."

"No matter how unimportant it seems to you it might seem important to us," said Cindy earnestly.

Mr. Crisp took off his spectacles and polished them. "I do remember some little thing, but it is too little to mention," he said, finally. "However, I will mention it. He asked me about our weather. He said that his caller—the other one from Kenoska—had a bad cold. He could not even recognize his voice. He could hardly understand him because he was talking in a whisper."

The whispering voice! thought Cindy, and she smiled. "It is important, Mr. Crisp. Thank you so much! You've helped us a lot with our mystery."

"But how could I help when I don't know anything?" asked Mr. Crisp.

Cindy looked at him steadily. "Mr. Crisp, *this* is important. If a Mr. Flamm—Mr. Harry Flamm, or a Mr. Chester Manchester tries to sell you some stamps, don't buy them. I can't explain why. But don't."

Cindy left Mr. Crisp shaking his head and looking puzzled. She was busy thinking that now she knew Mr. Manchester—Harry Flamm—had called Mr. Higginsby in New York last night. He had disguised his voice. He had whispered into the telephone. He had said he wanted to sell some rare stamps. Why? And why had he gone to a telephone booth? Why hadn't he called from the house?

# 8 · Mrs. Mudge Remembers

THE BOYS were cleaning up the branches from last night's storm at Road's End.

"When you're through with that, boys," called Mr. Manchester in his loud voice, "I have another job for you. Please empty the wastebaskets that I have set out in the back hallway. Empty them into the large trash cans behind the garage."

"Sure thing, Mr. Manchester," answered Dexter.

"Keep your eyes open, Dex!" whispered Jay.

"You bet," said Dexter.

In a few minutes Dexter walked in the back door. There were several wastebaskets on the floor.

All of them were filled with crumpled papers. Dexter looked quickly at the jacket and coat hanging on the pegs. And at the boots on the floor in the hallway. Cindy was right. There was no way the man who called himself Mr. Manchester could ever wear them.

Whose clothes were they? They looked quite new. They hadn't been left here by mistake by a former owner. They were expensive looking. Dexter peered more closely. There was a magazine in the pocket of the lightweight jacket.

Dexter pulled his glasses down on his nose. He reached into the pocket and took the magazine out. Quickly he looked at it. It was a weekly magazine, and it was dated just last week. Dexter turned the magazine around. The address label had the name Chester Manchester and the Kenoska address.

Dexter blinked. Whoever had worn that jacket had worn it last week. Who? The real Mr. Manchester? And where was he now?

Working fast, Dexter took the wastebaskets out to empty. He started to empty the wastebaskets into the trash cans. Several sheets of paper fell out, and he stooped to pick them up. They were covered with signatures!

The name *Chester Manchester* was written dozens and dozens of times. Dexter stared. Then he hastily stuffed one of the papers in his pocket.

Someone was coming. Dexter heard the footsteps. Dexter didn't have to guess who it was. He could hear the man walking toward him slowly. Quickly Dexter finished emptying the wastebaskets.

Had he seen Dexter put the paper in his pocket? Dexter whistled softly to cover his nervousness. Mr. Manchester was now standing beside him. Dexter turned around and smiled and nodded.

"All done, Mr. Manchester," he said. "Where do you want me to put the empty wastebaskets? Back in the hall?"

Mr. Manchester pulled on his moustache. He looked at Dexter with narrowed eyes. "No, I'll take them back," he decided. "That will be all. I'll pay you now."

"But we haven't finished, Mr. Manchester," protested Dexter, pushing his glasses up on his forehead. "There are still more branches."

"That's quite enough for now," said Mr. Manchester. "I can get my car out easily. We can get the other branches later."

He paid Dexter. "Give the other boy his share," he told Dexter.

"As if I wouldn't," thought Dexter to himself. He got Jay, and they started back to Mrs. Mudge's.

"I'm afraid he saw me put the paper in my pocket," whispered Dexter when they were out of sight.

"What paper?" asked Jay.

"I'll show you," promised Dexter. But Dexter didn't get a chance.

Cindy was waiting for them on the porch steps.

"Wait till I tell you what I found out!" she said.

She quickly told about Mr. Crisp and what he had told her about the New York buyer who wanted rare stamps. "The man in New York is Mr. Higginsby," she explained. "Mr. Crisp talked to him, too. He thought it was odd to get two calls from Kenoska. So now we know Mr. Manchester—really Harry Flamm—called him to sell stamps. Mr. Manchester's stamps!"

"Wait a minute," Jay said. "Mr. Hooley's rule. How do we know Mr. Flamm, if that's his real name, doesn't have Mr. Chester Manchester's permission to sell the stamps?"

Dexter drew the crumpled paper out of his pocket. "Look!" he said. "Here's the answer. There were lots of sheets like this in the wastebasket."

The three detectives huddled around the paper with the series of signatures. Dexter pulled his glasses down on his nose. He said slowly, "Harry Flamm is trying to forge the real Mr. Manchester's signature. That's what this paper has to mean."

They studied the page of writing. "See," said Jay, pointing. "The first ones are little and kind of cramped. Then they get more and more like the big scrawled one on Mrs. Spooner's letter." Jay took out his route book. "The first ones look like this one, like the way he signed that first day, Friday."

They all looked. "He is trying to imitate Chester Manchester's signature," said Dexter. "He's trying to pretend to be Chester Manchester. Why?"

"So that he can sell the stamps to Mr. Higginsby," Cindy said. "Mr. Higginsby must know the real Mr. Manchester. He must know his voice and the way he signs his name."

She looked up at Dexter and Jay.

"He pretended he was Chester Manchester on the telephone. Mr. Higginsby was used to Chester Manchester's voice. So Harry Flamm put a handkerchief over the mouthpiece. And he whispered. He pretended he had a cold, so Mr. Higginsby wouldn't realize that it was a different voice!"

Jay spoke up. "And he'll be selling the stamps to him. Pretending that he owns them. Pretending he is Chester Manchester! He's a crook!"

They stared at each other.

"We'll have to call Mr. Higginsby," said Jay. "He's got to be warned!"

"But the ad says to call Sunday nights only. And Mr. Crisp says that Mr. Higginsby travels a lot, and left this morning on a trip," said Cindy, frowning. "We can't reach him."

"Then we'll have to find the real Mr. Chester Manchester," said Jay. "We'll have to."

Dexter polished his glasses nervously. "We've got to tell him that someone has taken over his house. Someone has taken over his name and his signature."

"And his stamp collection," said Cindy gravely. "And selling it. Harry Flamm is selling it for thousands and thousands of dollars. And it doesn't belong to him!"

Dexter pushed his glasses up on his forehead. "What has he done with Mr. Manchester? That's what we have to find out—right away!"

"We must find him. Otherwise it will be too late," Jay went on. "Harry Flamm will have sold the stamps, got the money, and run away."

Dexter frowned. "Do you think he could be in the house? Maybe locked up, a prisoner?"

Jay shook his head. "I don't think so. His red sports car is gone. If he was a prisoner in the house, the pretend Mr. Manchester wouldn't even let us in the back hallway. He'd be afraid we'd hear or see something. He wouldn't let us in the yard."

"Maybe Mr. Manchester, the real Mr. Manchester, had to go away suddenly," guessed Dexter. "That gave Harry Flamm his chance."

"But where is he? Where has Chester Manchester gone?" wailed Cindy.

Just then Mrs. Mudge came out to the porch. "More fudge," she beamed.

"Mrs. Mudge," said Cindy. "We need your help. We know that the real Chester Manchester is not that man. That man is Harry Flamm. Now we have to find out where Mr. Manchester really is."

Mrs. Mudge shook her head. "I want to help you," she said. "But how?"

"Think of every single thing you've seen or heard that might be a clue," urged Jay.

Mrs. Mudge shook her head again, "I've told you everything. The way we joked about our names rhyming. You know, Mudge rhyming with fudge, Chester rhyming with Manchester." She pursed her lips and sat down on the swing. "I think better when I'm swinging," she confided. "It comes from reading all those mysteries out here."

She started to swing slowly back and forth. Suddenly she stopped swinging and looked up. "I thought of something. But of course it isn't anything important."

"What is it?" asked Dexter.

"Well, he did say that he had a brother in Los Angeles whose name rhymed, too. Lester. Lester and Chester Manchester."

She started to swing even more briskly. "Let me think, let me think," she said. "He said that, about the names. Lester and Chester, rhyme with each other, rhyme with Manchester. He said he had business with Lester, and he often flies out to California to see him." She sighed. "I'm afraid I just can't think of anything more."

The three detectives looked at Mrs. Mudge. Suddenly Jay snapped his fingers. "The red sports car had California license plates. Maybe Chester Manchester is there now!"

"And maybe Los Angeles has a billion people living there," said Dexter. "How could we find him?"

Jay nodded gloomily. "Talk about a needle in a haystack. That's what this is."

"It's worth a try," said Cindy, jumping up. "Can we use your telephone, Mrs. Mudge? We've got to call Los Angeles information. Let's see whether there is a Lester Manchester in Los Angeles."

"Let's all go in," said Mrs. Mudge. "It's so exciting."

They gathered around the kitchen table. "You talk, Cindy," said Jay.

Cindy picked up the telephone. She dialed Operator. "May I have Los Angeles, California, information?" she asked. The operator told her how to dial. In a moment Cindy was talking to another operator.

"Los Angeles directory service," said the voice. "May I help you?"

Cindy crossed her fingers. The boys copied her.

"Yes, please," said Cindy, swallowing. "Do you have a number for a Mr. Lester Manchester?"

"Manchester, ma'am?" asked the operator. "Lester Manchester?"

"Yes," said Cindy. "Lester Manchester."

"One moment please." The operator was silent.

Then she said, "I do have a Lester Manchester on Willow Drive."

"May I have that number, please?" asked Cindy nervously.

As the operator read the number, Cindy copied it. Then she read it back to the operator to be sure she had it right. Cindy hung up the telephone. "Maybe we'll find this needle in this haystack after all," she said excitedly.

Jay turned to Mrs. Mudge. "Can we call from here?" he asked. "We'll find out how much it costs and pay you back."

"Fine!" beamed Mrs. Mudge. "I can hardly wait! I'm so glad I'm in on all this!"

"I'm too nervous to call," said Cindy. "You call, Jay."

Jay scratched his head. "Well, okay, but stay close by, all of you. I may want you to talk, too."

"Let's make it a person-to-person call," said Dexter.

Jay picked up the telephone. He placed the call to Los Angeles. Mr. Lester Manchester's number. He let it ring and ring.

There was no answer.

# 9 · Warning by Long Distance

"BUT there has to be an answer!" cried Cindy. "There has to be!"

"We'll just have to try later, I guess," said Jay, hanging up.

"Let's try every few minutes," said Dexter. "We've got to find Chester Manchester. We've got to let him know about Harry Flamm."

They sat and looked at each other. Cindy leafed through her notebook.

"Of course we've got to be absolutely positively sure," she said. "We can't accuse him if he's innocent. Remember Mr. Hooley's rule."

"But we have proved it," said Jay. "We know he's not Mr. Manchester. We know he's pretending to be. Look at your notes! Look at the clues! It all adds up to the same thing: this man is an imposter. He's a fake!"

"And he's a crook," added Dexter, "trying to sell something that doesn't belong to him!"

"We have to stop him before he gets away with it," exclaimed Jay.

The three detectives kept calling the Los Angeles number. They called the rest of the afternoon. No luck.

When it was time to go home, Cindy said, "Mrs. Mudge, we'll come back tomorrow. We'll try phoning from home tonight. Keep watching!"

They tried again and again that night to reach the number. Finally they had to give it up until morning.

"Until *early* morning," said Jay. "Come over as soon as you can, Dex."

Early the next morning Dexter arrived at the Temple house.

"Good heavens, Dexter," said Mrs. Temple. "You're really early today. The early bird catches the worm! And from what Jay and Cindy have told me, there really is a worm to be caught." She laughed. "I'm just leaving for work. The kids are upstairs making the beds, I hope. Or have they gone back to sleep?" She put a hand behind her ear. "I think my lecture worked," she announced. "I hear movement. Not much, but a little. Have fun. I'll be waiting for a report tonight. Remember, you three pay for the long distance call."

"It will be worth it, Mrs. Temple," promised Dexter. "We'll really catch that worm."

"You can be sure it's the mystery that's got those two rolling, not my lecture," called Mrs. Temple as she went out to the car.

Jay and Cindy came hurrying downstairs.

"Let's call Mr. Manchester first," said Jay. "Breakfast can come later."

Cindy looked at her watch. "If it's eight o'clock here, it's only six o'clock in Los Angeles," she said. "Should we call this early?"

"Too early," said Jay. "I vote for breakfast."

"Me too," grinned Dexter. "How about pancakes, Cindy?"

Cindy made a face. "Pancakes sound fine," she said, "as long as you and Jay make them."

"Women's Lib," groaned Dexter. "I'll mix if you cook, how's that?"

"All right," agreed Cindy. "If Jay does the dishes."

After breakfast, the three detectives sat beside the telephone. "Cindy, you've looked at your watch ten times in the last ten minutes," said Dexter.

"And you've polished your glasses fifteen times," laughed Cindy.

"Let's call now," said Jay. "It's nine o'clock. That's seven o'clock there. If we wait, maybe he'll be gone."

"Maybe he's gone already," said Dexter.

"And maybe he's sound asleep," answered Cindy.

Jay swallowed. "Just because I said I'd be the one to talk, that doesn't mean that we can't change it."

"You are the one to talk," announced Dexter firmly. "We'll chime in if we have to. Go ahead, Jay. Now."

"Now or never," sighed Jay. He picked up the telephone.

"Let's dial direct," suggested Cindy. "Even if his brother Lester answers, he can tell us where Chester is, maybe."

Jay dialed. He heard the ring. Once. Twice. Three times.

"He's not home," said Jay finally. Then suddenly someone answered.

"Hello," said a man's sleepy voice.

"Hello, is this Mr. Manchester?" asked Jay.

Cindy poked Jay. "Ask if it's Chester or Lester," she said.

"Could I please speak to Chester or Lester Manchester?" asked Jay.

"Everyone is still sleeping here," said the voice on the other end. "Chester is sleeping, Lester is sleeping. Lester's cat, whose name I cannot recall, is sleeping. I suggest that you return this call at a more civilized hour. Until then, I bid you farewell."

Jay stared at the telephone for a split second. Then he said, "Oh, please don't hang up. It's very important!"

The voice said, "My friend, nothing is important at this hour of the morning. Nothing but sleep."

"Be firm," whispered Cindy, whose ear was pressing against Jay's.

"I must talk to Mr. Manchester. It's very important," urged Jay.

The voice sighed. "Which Mr. Manchester?"

"Mr. Chester Manchester," said Jay.

The voice sighed again. "I am Mr. Chester. But I warn you, whoever you are, that if this is *not* important that I will personally draw and quarter you, wherever you might be."

Jay looked at the telephone. Then he looked at Cindy and at Dexter. "Help!" he whispered.

Cindy handed him the notebook. Jay glanced at it and nodded. Then he said into the telephone, "Mr. Manchester, my name is Jay Temple. I'm from Kenoska. And someone is in your house. His name is Harry Flamm. He's whispering. He wouldn't let Mrs. Spooner in. He signed my route book the wrong way."

Jay looked at Cindy's notes. "He doesn't know the difference between Frisco and Tomtom. The clothes don't fit him."

The voice yawned. "It's okay, it's okay. It's Harry. Old Harry Flamm. Of course he's in my house. He's there because I asked him to stay while I was away. Any other problem I can solve for you?"

"You asked him to be there?" asked Jay. He stared at the telephone.

"Of course," yawned the voice. "Everything is fine. Why don't we all go back to bed?"

"Tell him about the signature," said Cindy.

"Mr. Manchester," said Jay. "This Harry Flamm is pretending to be you. He's signing your name and everything. I mean, he's practicing it."

"Let me talk," said Dexter. He took the telephone.

"He may be your friend, Mr. Manchester, but he's not honest," said Dexter.

"He's not my friend," yawned the voice. "He's my cousin."

Cindy grabbed the telephone. "He's an imposter!"

"Look," said the sleepy voice. "I don't know who you are, and I don't know why your voice changes every few minutes. It's something I will solve later."

"Please listen, Mr. Manchester!" continued Cindy. "It's terribly, terribly important."

"Wait a minute," said the voice. "Don't go away. Just sit there. Let me get a cup of coffee."

"He's paying attention," said Cindy. "That's all we need. Take the phone, Jay. I'm exhausted."

In a few minutes the voice was back.

"The coffee is plugged in, but it's not done yet," it said. "Don't say anything important until I've had a cup. Meantime, tell me about what's been happening. Who are you, by the way?"

"I'm Jay Temple. I'm your newsboy," said Jay. "My sister and my friend and I have a detective club. We knew something was wrong. Right from the beginning."

"Well, now, let's be sensible," said the voice. "Mysteries are easily solved if you know the facts. I'll tell you my facts first. I am Mr. Chester Manchester. I have bought a house there in Kenoska, Illinois, a nice house, where I hope to spend many happy years. My needs are small, my needs are few. I have my books, I have my friends, I have my stamps, I have my dogs. I have everything. Everything but this cup of coffee which I am about to have. Hold on."

There was another silence.

"What is he saying?" whispered Dexter, polishing his glasses.

"Nothing, so far," answered Jay. "He's getting a cup of coffee."

"Getting a cup of coffee? Long distance?" asked Cindy.

In a moment Mr. Manchester's voice said, "Now, young man, you say something seemed wrong? Just what seemed wrong? Start at the very beginning, please. Don't begin at the end. It's confusing."

Jay looked at Cindy's notes.

"Well, the first thing was that he didn't remember about Mrs. Spooner's coming on Friday."

The voice sighed. "I forgot to tell him. Let me explain."

Cindy and Dexter tried to press their ears against the telephone.

"Harry Flamm is my cousin. I don't know him very well. But cousins are cousins. One tries to be a cousin whenever possible. Harry Flamm had a business venture that he wanted to discuss with me. I agreed that he might come to visit me. Just as I moved in."

There was a pause as Mr. Manchester sipped his coffee. Cindy groaned. "Long distance sipping!"

The voice continued. "The day he arrived, I was called away. Here to Los Angeles. I had just

moved into the house in Kenoska. The house was not settled. I had the dogs to care for. But I had to come to Los Angeles."

Another pause. Another sip of coffee.

"So as long as he was there, I asked Harry Flamm if he could stay, just for a day or so. I couldn't leave the dogs alone, you see. And I couldn't bring them with me."

Another sip, another pause.

"And I don't like kennels because the dogs don't."

Jay held the telephone tightly.

"I came out here. I found I had to stay a few days longer than I had planned. Harry agreed to remain until I returned. To take care of Frisco and Tomtom."

"But he isn't taking care of them. He sent them to a kennel!" said Jay.

"Well, perhaps he isn't used to dogs," the voice continued. "When you know the facts, a mystery disappears. Harry Flamm didn't remember the dogs' names. Harry Flamm didn't know of my talk with

Mrs. Mudge. Harry Flamm didn't want Mrs. Spooner working there. Thought she'd be nosey, I suppose. That's all. That's the end of the mystery."

Jay stared at the telephone, and then at Dexter and Cindy. "But Mr. Manchester," he said. "There's much more than that!"

Dexter grabbed the telephone.

"Mr. Manchester," he said, "you say your cousin Harry Flamm came to see you about a business proposition. While he was there, you got word that you had to go to Los Angeles."

The voice interrupted. "I hear you saying things I already know," he said.

"But after you left, Harry Flamm started to pretend he was you. He started to practice signing your name. He whispered on the telephone in case anyone called who knew your voice."

Cindy reached for the telephone.

"He's selling your stamps, Mr. Manchester! Harry Flamm is selling your stamps."

"He was just visiting," said the voice sleepily, "and when I had to go away I asked him if . . ."

The voice paused. "What did you say? What did you say—about the stamps?"

"He's selling them, Mr. Manchester," said Cindy.

There was another pause. Then "Oh, no, he's not!" said Mr. Manchester's voice.

"He is, Mr. Manchester, he is," repeated Cindy.

"Look, where are you now?" asked Mr. Manchester.

"We're at home," explained Cindy. "We're a mile or so from your house."

There was a muffled exclamation.

"I'll come right away. I'll get a flight out this morning. I'll be there this afternoon. Don't let him leave. Don't let him leave with my stamps!"

Mr. Manchester had hung up.

# 10 · One Slip of the Tongue

THE THREE DETECTIVES sat staring at the telephone.

Suddenly Dexter jumped up. "Let's go!" he said. "We've got to watch Harry Flamm. We've got to see that he doesn't leave—with the stamps."

They ran outside and jumped on their bikes. Soon they were wheeling into Mrs. Mudge's driveway.

"Oh, I'm glad you came now," she said. "I have to get my new glasses. I was afraid you'd come while I was gone. Did you ever get Mr. Manchester on the telephone?"

"Just now," explained Jay quickly. "And he's on his way!"

"On his way here?" asked Mrs. Mudge, looking from one to the other. "Dear me! How exciting!"

"He said he'd take a flight right away. It's only a few hours away. He'll be here by late this afternoon," said Dexter, pulling his glasses down on his nose.

"We told him all about Harry Flamm," said Cindy. "And about his pretending to be Chester Manchester. About his trying to sell Mr. Manchester's stamps."

"Mr. Manchester told us to be sure he didn't leave—with the stamps," added Dexter.

"Oh no!" said Mrs. Mudge, looking stricken.

"What's wrong?" asked Cindy.

"Why, he *has* gone. He left a few minutes ago. Drove away in that gray car."

The three detectives stared at Mrs. Mudge.

"We've missed him," wailed Cindy.

"He must have known we were on to him," said Jay.

"Maybe he did see me put that piece of paper with those signatures in my pocket!" groaned Dexter.

They sat down on the porch steps. "We solved the mystery. But the criminal got away," said Jay.

"Maybe not," said Mrs. Mudge comfortingly.

"Maybe he just went out on an errand. He probably doesn't even know you suspect him."

Cindy brightened. "That's right," she said. "He was planning to leave on Wednesday. Well, this is only Tuesday. Maybe you're right, Mrs. Mudge. Maybe he will be back."

"He really couldn't guess that we'd found all that out about him," said Jay after a minute.

"Let's hope," said Dexter. "Let's wait here until he gets back."

"*If* he gets back," added Cindy.

"I'll fix us something to eat while we're waiting," said Mrs. Mudge, bustling into the house.

It was a long morning. And a long afternoon.

"We've missed him," said Cindy for the tenth time.

"We were so close, too," added Jay gloomily.

"Look!" hissed Dexter suddenly. "Here comes his car!"

Sure enough. Coming slowly down the street was the big gray car. Mr. Harry Flamm was at the wheel.

"Thank heaven," breathed Cindy. "We haven't lost him at all."

"Now all we have to do is to make sure he doesn't leave again until Mr. Manchester gets here," said Jay.

"Maybe he's been out selling the stamps," suggested Jay.

"Well, even if he has, he hasn't had a chance to spend all that money," said Dexter, pushing his glasses up on his forehead.

They watched as Harry Flamm got out of his car. He opened the gate. Then he drove slowly into his driveway.

"He didn't shut the gate behind him," whispered Jay.

"Maybe he's going right out again," said Dexter. "Maybe going for good next time."

"Well, we can't go over there. We can't let him know that we suspect anything," said Cindy. "How can we find out what he's going to do?"

Mrs. Mudge started to swing back and forth very fast. "I have an idea," she said finally. "A way that one of you could go over there, to make sure he's not planning a getaway this afternoon."

"What is it?" asked Cindy quickly.

"One of the boys could take Mrs. Spooner's

bag over there. She's to start work this week, remember. It would save her having to carry it. It could be there when she got there. You could explain that to Mr. Manchester. To Harry Flamm, I mean."

"That's a great idea," exclaimed Dexter. "Where is the bag?"

"In the living room," answered Mrs. Mudge.

Dexter ran into the house. In a moment he was outside with the big bag. "I'll try to find out whether he has any plans to leave today," he announced.

"Be careful! He'd leave in a minute if he thought we suspected him," said Cindy.

Mrs. Mudge watched him. "Oh, dear," she said, "I'm going to have to leave in just a few minutes."

Dexter walked with the bag over to the gate. Then he turned and waved to Jay and Cindy.

"I have a funny feeling that something bad is going to happen," frowned Cindy.

"Don't be silly," said Jay. "What could happen?"

"I just feel it in my bones," said Cindy.

"What could possibly happen with all of us sitting right here?" asked Jay.

"I have to go to pick up my new glasses," said Mrs. Mudge, looking at her watch. "I hope nothing exciting happens while I'm gone."

Jay and Cindy watched Mrs. Mudge until she was out of sight. Then they stared at the open gate at Road's End. And waited.

Dexter carried the bag up to the front door. He rang the doorbell. He rang again. There was no answer.

Maybe Harry Flamm was in the garage, thought Dexter. He walked around to the back of the house. And sure enough, Harry Flamm was putting something into the trunk of his car.

"Hello, Mr. Manchester," said Dexter when he saw him.

Harry Flamm jumped and turned around. His long hair was in his eyes. "What do you want?" he asked, brushing his hair away.

Dexter held up Mrs. Spooner's bag. "I thought I could bring this over for Mrs. Spooner," he explained. "She left it at Mrs. Mudge's. She keeps her cleaning supplies in here. Mrs. Mudge didn't want it cluttering up her house."

"I don't believe it," he said.

Dexter's heart pounded. Had he seen through Dexter's excuse? Did he know that Dexter knew he was Harry Flamm?

"You don't believe it?" asked Dexter, trying to think of something to say.

"I don't believe she keeps cleaning supplies in it," said Harry Flamm. "I think she would probably fill it full of household treasures. I never trust anyone who carries a bag to work."

Dexter breathed a sigh of relief. Harry Flamm went on. "However, put it out in the back hallway. And as long as you're here, I have a job for you to do first. I have a couple of suitcases and some boxes that I want you to put in my car. I'm going away tomorrow."

Dexter swallowed. Harry Flamm had said "tomorrow." Dexter hoped he was telling the truth. How could he find out for sure? Dexter thought quickly. "Would you rather I came back tomorrow and did it then? I'll be working on Mrs. Mudge's lawn."

Harry Flamm pulled at his moustache. "I want to get away early. By seven or eight," he said. "We may as well load the car now. Come on, I'll show you where the things are."

Dexter followed Harry Flamm into the house. There were two suitcases and three boxes in the middle of the living room. On a nearby couch was a briefcase.

"You'll have to make two trips," said Harry Flamm, pushing his hair out of his eyes.

Dexter started out to the car.

On his second trip to the garage, Dexter carried the briefcase. Suddenly Harry Flamm strode across the driveway and snatched it from Dexter's grasp. "Not that!" he growled. "That stays with me!"

Dexter was startled. Suddenly he realized that the stamps must be in the briefcase. No wonder Harry Flamm wanted to keep it near him.

Dexter finished putting the suitcases and boxes into the car. Then he picked up Mrs. Spooner's bag and started to the back hallway with it. He'd learned two things, anyway. Harry Flamm wasn't leaving until tomorrow. And the stamps were in the briefcase.

Dexter sighed with relief. Mr. Manchester would be coming pretty soon now. He would deal with Harry Flamm.

If it hadn't been for the Spotlight Club, Harry

Flamm would have stolen Chester Manchester's stamps!

Dexter carried the bag to the hallway. Harry Flamm had followed him to the back door and stood there. Dexter set the heavy bag down and then he turned around. Harry Flamm was standing in the doorway.

"Is there anything else, then, Mr. Flamm?" asked Dexter. As soon as he had said it, he realized his mistake. He'd called him Mr. Flamm.

Harry Flamm stared at Dexter.

"You know, do you?" he snarled. "You little sneak!"

He started toward Dexter. Then suddenly he stopped. "I'll be back to deal with you!" he said. He turned and slammed the door.

Dexter heard the bolt. Quickly Dexter ran to the other door, the door that led into the house. It was locked.

Dexter was locked in the back hallway.

And Harry Flamm knew Dexter knew his secret. What would he do now?

Dexter stood and listened, his heart pounding. Was Harry Flamm going to come back and open the hallway door? What would he do to Dexter?

Dexter listened. He heard Harry Flamm run around the house to the front door.

He could hear him walking in the house. He could hear his voice. He must be telephoning someone.

Dexter waited. No one would hear him if he called for help. Only Harry Flamm.

What would he do to Dexter?

Cindy and Jay were waiting for Dexter at Mrs. Mudge's. She hadn't come back yet, either.

"What's happened to Dexter?" worried Cindy. "He's been gone a long time."

"Oh, he's okay," said Jay. "He'll just keep an eye on Harry Flamm. One thing we know for sure— Harry Flamm won't leave. Dexter won't let him. We don't have a thing to worry about."

Cindy peered over at the gate.

Suddenly they heard the sound of a car starting. Harry Flamm's car. Harry Flamm was leaving.

Jay sprang to his feet. At the same moment, Cindy started to run over to the gate.

"Shut the gate!" yelled Jay.

The car had backed out of the garage. Cindy

slammed the gate shut. At the same moment, Jay reached for the chain that was hanging on the gatepost. In a moment he had started wrapping it around the gate.

The car was heading in their direction. Suddenly the brakes were slammed on hard as Harry Flamm saw the closed gate.

"Hurry up, Jay," urged Cindy.

"There's no way to lock it," said Jay breathlessly. Harry Flamm sprang out of the car and ran toward them. He reached across the gate and grabbed Jay. Cindy quickly climbed over the gate. She ran up behind Harry Flamm and tried to pull him away from Jay.

"Get Dexter!" shouted Jay to Cindy, as he was struggling with Harry Flamm.

Harry Flamm turned to grab Cindy. She broke away and ran to the house.

"Dexter!" she shouted. "Where are you? Help! Harry Flamm's going to hurt Jay! He's going to get away!"

Suddenly she heard Dexter shouting. She ran toward the sound of his voice.

"In the back hallway!" shouted Dexter.

Cindy ran to the back door. It was bolted. Quickly she threw open the bolt. Dexter pushed the door open.

"Hurry!" she urged.

They ran down the driveway to the gate. Jay had fallen beside the gate. Cindy saw blood on his head. Harry Flamm was running toward his car.

Jay sat up, shaking his head. Blood trickled down his face. "Don't let him go!" he shouted.

Harry Flamm saw Dexter and Cindy running toward him. Jay stumbled to his feet, trying to hold the gate shut. Harry Flamm reached inside his car and grabbed the briefcase. He tried to push the gate open. Jay held tight. Harry Flamm swung the brief-case and knocked Jay down. Then he wheeled around to face Dexter and Cindy.

Dexter saw the man reach for his pocket. He drew out a small pocketknife and opened it.

"Get back," Harry Flamm warned.

"Be careful, Cindy," yelled Jay.

Suddenly there was the sound of brakes screeching to a stop. It was a police car.

A voice shouted, "Hold it! Hold it, Harry Flamm! It's the police!"

Harry Flamm froze in his tracks.

A taxi pulled up behind the police car. A short bald man jumped out. It was Chester Manchester, the real Chester Manchester.

Everything happened so quickly that, as Cindy said later, she didn't know what was going on until it was all over.

After the police had left with Harry Flamm, Chester Manchester told the three detectives that Harry had taken the stamps. And not only the stamps, but some other valuable things as well.

Chester Manchester shook his head. "Harry's always been a different sort of person," he said. "Black sheep and all that. I thought maybe he'd straightened out. But I guess he hasn't."

Chester Manchester had invited the three detectives and Mrs. Mudge for supper, and Mrs. Mudge volunteered to bring a casserole.

The two dogs had been brought from the kennel, and they sat at Mr. Manchester's feet. Now Cindy had her notebook in her lap.

"I think you figured it all out," said Chester Manchester. "Harry Flamm decided after I left that he could pretend to be me. That way he could sell my stamps."

Jay nodded. "I think I know when he decided he could pretend to be you," he said. "I remember when I first met him I called him Mr. Manchester. He started to say 'I'm not—' and then he must have decided, 'Well, why not?' That's when he signed your name in my route book."

"I've been wondering why he used the telephone booth," said Cindy. "He could have called from here. Of course it's lucky he didn't. That was our main clue."

Chester Manchester smiled over at Cindy and rubbed Frisco's head. "At that point he thought he could get away with selling the stamps without my knowing about it. I had just moved here, you know, and things were still in a state of disorder. It might have been months before I'd notice any stamps were missing. And by then many people would have been coming and going. There would have been no way for me to prove it was Harry Flamm."

He looked around the room. "He didn't want any long distance calls on my telephone bill when I got back," he explained. "Especially numbers that I would recognize. Like Higginsby's."

He shook his head. "He hadn't planned this ahead. He made it all up as he went along," he continued. "He got the idea when I was called out of town and when Jay thought he was Chester Manchester. He thought he could get away with it."

The doorbell rang.

"I'll get it," offered Cindy.

She opened the door. A tall thin lady in a red hat stood there. She peered down at Cindy.

It was Mrs. Spooner. Pointing at Cindy she demanded, "And where is Chester Manchester?"

Mr. Manchester came to the door. "May I help you?" he asked.

Mrs. Spooner blinked. "No, I want to see Mr. Manchester," she said.

"I am he," said Mr. Manchester.

She shook her head. "I mean the other one."

Mr. Manchester smiled. "There's been a mix-up," he said.

She nodded briskly. Her mouth turned down. "You're right. A mixup. I'm Mrs. Spooner. Hired by Chester Manchester. Well, I'm out of this job! It's a crazy place! Crazy! I've taken another position. Now I've come for my bag. That lady next door says it's here."

"I'll get it," said Dexter quickly. He ran out through the kitchen to the back hallway. When he looked at the hall he smiled to himself. It didn't look scary now. But it had earlier today! He picked up the bag and brought it into the living room.

"Put it in the taxi," said Mrs. Spooner, pointing

to Dexter. He grinned to himself as he carried the bag outside.

After Mrs. Spooner had left, they sat once more in the living room.

"You've all been very clever," said Mr. Chester Manchester. "You put many difficult clues together to come up with the answer."

"We couldn't have done it without Mrs. Mudge," said Cindy. "She was the one who told us you had a brother in Los Angeles. Otherwise we'd never have been able to find you until it was too late."

Chester Manchester nodded. "A fine woman," he said.

At that moment the doorbell rang. It was Mrs. Mudge. "With the casserole," she announced. "And rolls. And cake. And fudge!"

"Mrs. Mudge," said Chester Manchester. "Could you come over once in a while with casseroles and fudge?"

"As often as you like!" beamed Mrs. Mudge.

"Maybe once in a while you could tidy up? Then I wouldn't need a Mrs. Spooner."

"I'd love to!" said Mrs. Mudge happily. "But

I have no references. I've never worked before!"

"You have all the references I need," answered Chester Manchester, glancing around the room at the three detectives.

Suddenly they heard a door slam outside. "Another visitor?" asked Chester Manchester, raising his eyebrows.

This time he went to the door. There was a long conversation. Cindy craned her neck to see who it was.

Mr. Crisp! Chester Manchester brought him into the living room and introduced him. When he saw Cindy, he nodded and waved.

"You were very helpful, young lady," he said. "Remember, you told me not to buy any stamps from a Chester Manchester? Well, he came in today." He smiled and corrected himself. "At least he *said* he was Chester Manchester. I learn now that he was not. Anyway, I did not buy his stamps, thanks to you, young lady. But I pretended I was interested. I got his address. I was coming out here today. I was eager to learn what I could. If he was really a fraud, I wanted to know about it. I wanted to warn other stamp dealers."

He tapped his cane on the floor and went on.

"I was delayed. He called me and was angry. Said he had to leave right away. Was I coming or not?" Mr. Crisp shrugged his shoulders. "I came, but he was gone. I have just learned why."

Dexter nodded. "That's why he waited so long after he locked me in the hallway. He was waiting for Mr. Crisp to come to buy some stamps. To have enough money to leave with!"

Chester Manchester nodded. "A good job well done," he smiled at the detectives.

They smiled at each other.

"Mrs. Mudge, perhaps Mr. Crisp will join us for that casserole," beamed Chester Manchester. "And perhaps you will enjoy looking at some of my most prized stamps, Mr. Crisp."

"I'll set another place," smiled Mrs. Mudge.

"I can't resist," said Mr. Crisp. "My two favorite things, stamps and dinner!"

Cindy held up her notebook. "Another mystery solved. The mystery of Chester Manchester. I mean Harry Flamm. What a book it turned out to be!"

"And what a crook he turned out to be," said Jay.

"Dinner's ready," announced Mrs. Mudge.

"And what a cook you turned out to be, Mrs. Mudge," laughed Dexter.

"What do you think the next mystery's going to be?" asked Cindy.

"That's another day," said Jay, grinning. "Another day, another book, and maybe another crook."

"But another meal is here and ready. First things first," said Dexter.

They all laughed as they sat down to dinner.